Where They Lay

Eve Elderwell

Published by Eve Elderwell, 2023.

This is a work of fiction. Similarities to real people, places, or events are entirely coincidental.

WHERE THEY LAY

First edition. July 31, 2023.

ISBN: 979-8223929963

Written by Eve Elderwell.

Dedicated to the women in my family, those still with us and those crossed over. May we continue to heal, to nurture creativity, and to support each other on our life journeys.

Where They Lay

My Dearest Janice,

Well, I promised you I'd write you a story before my time had come and gone, so that's what I'm settin' about to do. Pay no mind to the shaky lettering or the misspelling of my punctuation—my hands can't quite write what my head thinks anymore—and even then, I question my mind's motives!

It's about time I tell you a little something even my ole Jake didn't know about! Come now—I can see you scrunchin' your brow already—but believe me you, if ever you get married—which saddens me that I won't be there to witness that future lucky man and warn him that if ever he lays a hand in vain on my granddaughter I'll.. well, never mind, I digress...if ever you <u>do</u> cut the cake with a man lassoed to your ring finger, why honey, you'll realize that even after some 50 odd years of marriage there will still be some things your hubby will never know about you.

Now that ain't a bad thing, sweetie, mark my words—a little intrigue always keeps things spicy in the bedroom—oh yes, my old man and me still had quite the time together even when we smelled like mothballs and couldn't remember if he'd taken the 'magic pill' or not! Why, there *was* this one time during an absolutely dreadful community band concert at Jake's assisted care center that Jake feigned an attack of chest pain and we snuck off to…

Oh blast it all, my memories are taking me on a road trip today!

No Janice, Jake didn't know everything about me, at least not what I'm about to share with you. Before you read any further, you may want to finish that nice glass of Zinfandel I'm sure you're holding and cozy up with Rascal on the couch since I highly doubt you'll be leaving the house by the time I'm through with you!

Setting down my grandmother's letter, my fingers tremble slightly as I reach for my glass of red Zin. Her letter is dated May 13th, three days before her passing, and it's taken me 10 times that long to find the courage to read her last words ever written. Granny always used to read me bed-time stories that she had written herself when I was a child; truth be told, I knew the envelope I received after her funeral contained a story.

Her sealed final words vibrated like a firefly in a Mason Jar when I first held that envelope. I just hadn't been ready to smell her Eau de Parfum or lift her script to my face—until now.

"Janice, sooner or later, you have to tear open that envelope like you're tearing off a bandage," Nick, my boyfriend and paramedic at the UNC Specialty Care hospital here in Pittsboro, North Carolina, told me the other day. "Or else, your grief will fester and become infected with fear."

He has a point, I begrudgingly admit, so on a sweltering Friday night I find myself home alone – again, because when does any post-grad student struggling to pay off vet school loans by working two jobs have any time for a social life??—save for another hot date with a suitor flaunting the name Zin, a chaperone by the name of Rascal the Cat, and an old, frumpy, second-hand floral couch having seen better days. I must admit though, it makes for an acceptable bed when I fall asleep after binging on Netflix while Jake works graveyard at the hospital.

Holy heavens to Betsy—how could Granny have pegged me so accurately? It's like she knew even before she met God above what I'd be doing when I finally told the coward within to take a hike and forced myself to open her letter tonight.

And if she has her way too, there's no chance I'm going anywhere soon if she's fixin' to tell me a story that will knock me out like a sleeping pill—or better yet, a bottle of wine.

I oughta pour me another glass, then.

Now sugar, don't be getting your hopes up too high here...this story goes back to a time before I knew Jake. Oh yes, the year was 1950 and Pittsboro, North Carolina, was so small a deer coulda mistaken it for a nice place to leave a pile of dung. Your grandmother was the talk of the town, and if you could believe it or not, this here ole southern belle used to look mighty fine in her New Look A-style dress walking down Main Street with her girlfriend Sally after church. If I dare say so myself, all the young men came a-callin' soon as I graduated from high school.

"Miz Liza-belle, fancy a ride in my new Thunderbird?"

That was the banker's boy.

"Miss Eliza, would you be so kind as to join me for an evening of Jitterbug at the City Hall this Saturday night?" The shoemaker's son, he never could take no for an answer. Polite as a dime, even though his two front teeth were horribly scrunched together and his fine red-headed complexion always blistered like a bruised peach in the hot summer sun.

But no...no matter how sweet, flatterin', and smart-like these boys acted around me, they never could wrangle my attention away from one young man in particular.

Joshua Jones.

Maybe it was the way he greeted me every time I walked into Ray's Pharmacy to purchase 5 cent lollipops and gumdrops.

"How do you do, miss," he'd tip his hat at me and smile so wide I dare say I saw the moon nestled in his molars. Or perhaps it was the way he'd attend to the door as I carried my purchases out of the store.

"You have a mighty fine day now, ya hear miss Liza?"

Or maybe it was the musk I'd walk through as I'd breeze past him—the smell of the sun, sweat, and tobacco lingerin' in the air between us. He certainly smelled better than the Dior cologne my father wore to the office, and he certainly didn't smell the way the other young men my age smelt, more like cheap booze and diner food on a night out to the movies.

Honestly, if I speak from the bones of my belly, it was the way he looked at me, as if I were really someone special. As if just seeing me would light up his day.

"Come back again soon, miss Liza," he'd say.

Come now, Janice, I know what you're thinking, and I'll tell ya what: guess where your good looks come from? Underneath this flappy tummy the size of Georgia and wrinkles that put the

Grand Canyon to shame is a woman who still remembers what it felt like to have all the young men eyeing her every time she went to a Saturday night Dance Social at City Hall. It's the *babies*, I tell ya, the babies that'll do ya in. And when I popped out 3 of them before I ever saw 25, why, that'll age ya like a cucumber boiled in pickling brine! I know all you young ladies just want one thing: a little one to dress up and coo over, but at my age, I see the silly old bats here act the same way over their hairy little white dogs as they do a baby.

So wait, child, just you wait until after you marry and have a little fun with your hubby before you go asking for the smell of stained milk on your shirt and dark eye circles on your cheeks for the next 18 years of your life. That'll sure age your arse quickly...

Whoops! Did I just curse? How ungodly of me—must be those ladies at the weekly game of Cards and Bridge that the nurses insist I attend. They test my patience till the cows come home, and that's why I never could marry me a farmer.

Now bless your heart, Janice, I've about put you to sleep by now, I reckon. I've about worn my slap out too tryin' to write this all while this baggy body suit is still breathing...

What say you I take me a little nap before lunch and I'll pick up from where I've left off after my blood sugar is stable again?

Bzzz bzzz. The text message alert on my phone vibrates on the table, breaking my concentration. Even Rascal lifts his long-haired head from his spot on my lap in surprise.

I set the papers aside, reach for the phone: Nick's just texted me.

Hey babe, I'm on a quick break. You hangin' in there?

So far so good. I've just started reading Granny's letter

Got a glass of wine to help you through it?

Why does everyone assume I'll need wine to read her letter? But yes, I do

Because you would have opened it sooner if you weren't afraid of what you'd find inside

Touché

I have a nasty habit of chewing on my lower lip when I'm tired, stressed, or sad. This is one of those moments. **How's your night?**

Slow. Should get off early. If you need me, I can swing by when I get out

I'll let you know. Thanks

Rascal mews for attention, and I oblige by setting down my phone and scratching him under the chin. Tufts of hair scatter through the air and land on the hand-knit, threadbare pink blanket Granny made me. Granny practically raised my brothers and I when my parents divorced, and we came to love the days Granny came over with a home-made peach pie and sweet tea. She often knit me socks, sweaters, or scarves. For my 10th birthday, she knit me this blanket, and after her funeral, I pulled it out of my closet to use as a cover-up on my equally worn-out and ratty couch.

Oh God, I don't know if I can keep reading. The words are swimming in front of my eyes, and it's not just from the alcohol. Picking up her letter once more, I take the last swig from my glass and start reading again.

It all started at the Chatham County Fair that summer in 1950. I had just graduated from high school, and at that point, I was more interested in keepin' up with the latest fashion trends, singin' along to Doris Day, and wonderin' if a bob or a perm made my face look older than I was in the increasin' social unrest occurring around me.

Now mind you, Janice, the civil rights movement may seem like it was way before your time, but I lived through it just like your generation lived through 9/11. When I was in school, blacks still went to schools for the colored. Holy tarnation, everything was still divided—there were neighborhoods for the blacks, restrooms for the blacks, even bubblers for the blacks.

That summer, there were rumors that the Gov'ner of North Carolina was participatin' in a Civil Action Committee to discuss the desegregation of all public spaces, includin' schools, but most people in Pittsboro were strongly opposed. There was a heightened tension in the air, and even an occasional rally as white people, mostly white men, gathered in protest against the anti-segregation laws "forced upon us" by those "soft-bellied, wussie, stuck up politicians" in the North.

But nope, I was still a clueless lassie with my curls in the clouds and my cuticles covered in satin gloves, scarcely noticin' the commotion brewin' around me.

That day at the fair, I was lookin' mighty fine too—I was all dolled up in a new sunhat and striped jumper mother had let me order from the <u>catalog</u>. She had even let me wear rouge and a dab of her Lancôme perfume!

"Sally-belle, I fancy me an ice-cream cone," I announced as we flounced out of the arcade.

My best friend from high school tossed her blonde curls over her shoulders and assumed an exaggerated pout.

"Mother says I need to be watchin' my waist this summer—what with the summer pageant approachin', I can't be competin' lookin' like a brown bear with its head stuck in the honey jar."

Beauty queens, I tell ya Janice, they may talk with their teeth coated in sugar, but on the inside, they're just as rotten as the rest of us.

"Well, you might be watchin' your figure, but I'm still tryin' to grow my bust out to look like yours," so I grabbed her wrist in a particularly unladylike fashion and half-dragged her across the swelterin' fairgrounds, oblivious to her weak little whimpers of protest.

And it's then that I saw him.

Oh Janice, I swear he made my insides melt like a stick of butter in a frying pan. He was workin' the ice cream cart, lookin' so pert and smart with his red apron tied about his waist and his name sewn in white thread across the black cotton of his tee shirt.

But it was too late to stop now, so I timidly approached the cart, lettin' go of Sally's waist to search for a spare quarter in the front flap of my jumper. Sally stood off to the side, rubbin' her wrist and makin' a point of sighin' heavily and loudly.

But I paid her no mind.

"Miss Liza, fancy seeing you here!" and when Joshua lifted his eyes to meet mine, a wide grin formin' little crinkles around the corners of his eyes, my heart just about fell out of my mouth my jaw must've been open so wide.

I shut my trap like I'd just caught me a bullfrog and squared my shoulders as if his appearance hadn't startled the livin' bejeebers out of me.

"Hello Joshua, it's a mighty fine day for a fair," I croaked.

"Indeed it is, indeed it is," he replied, brilliant white teeth blindin' me as strongly as the sun. "And a mighty fine day for some ice-cream. Can I interest you lovely young ladies in something special, perhaps a root beer float? I even have birch beer too—it tastes great with a scoop of cherry ice cream," he winked.

"Nothing for me," Sally scoffed, her attention focused on correctin' her dark red lipstick in her hand-held mirror, payin' us no mind.

"I'm just hankerin' for an ice cream cone," I spluttered. "I'll take a chocolate and vanilla twist, please."

"Chocolate and vanilla, eh? That's one of my favorites too," he winked again, and I looked away, blushin'. Nearby, Sally was tappin' her foot impatiently, looking tired and bored. She wouldn't admit it, but she secretly wanted to run into Billy Niles again—he was set to ship out with the military later that summer, and she was hopin' he'd take her along. He was wanderin' around the campground somewhere with his buddies no doubt, probably eatin' some fried chicken and shootin' some darts.

"Here ya go, Miss Liza," Joshua's voice warbled through my wavy perm and caressed my earlobe. "This one's on me this time."

And as he passed me my wafer cone, the chocolate and vanilla twisted around one another like long-lost lovers, his fingers grazed against mine. We both froze, eyes locked, an electric charge surging between our fingertips—and for one perfect moment in time, my cool, milky white skin interlaced with the warmth of his solid, black fingers.

"You have a good day now, ya hear Miss Liza?" He finally pulled away, and I was left there for the second time that day flounderin' like a fish out of water.

"I'll be seeing you," he tipped his hat, winked once more, and turned away to help the Jenkin's boys waitin' next in line.

"Are you done yet?" Sally had marched back up, makeup freshly re-applied. "I'm hungry," she announced. "Let's go check out the food carts; I told Billy I'd meet him at half-past four, so we mustn't be late." Now it was her turn to grab me by the arm, beauty queen or not, and stomp unceremoniously back the way we came looking for a hot meal to fill her belly—or better yet: a teenage love to fill her heart. I think I'd just gotten me a taste of that, and I was starvin'.

Holy bucket of oats, I think I need another glass. Halfway through the bottle, and her story's only just begun. I can only imagine what Gramps woulda thought if Granny had ever shared this story with him while he was still alive. He woulda run out of the elder home in nothing but his diapers, cussing and screaming for the lord to take him then and there. I wonder what else she's got hiding up her knickers. Sweet peaches and cream, if

I knew I'd be reading a chick flick I woulda opened this letter weeks ago.

Now Janice, how do you go about explaining to a naïve little white girl that harborin' a crush on a colored boy coulda gotten her sent to finishing school in the deep south—or worse yet, married off to the first suitor who came a-callin' faster than you could say "scatcataboodlybat"? You oughta see how these ladies around here ooh and aah every time Obama comes on TV, coddling about saying, "aren't Obama's daughters just the cutest things in their lacy white gowns? And Michelle in her pin-up, why..?"

Oh no, on Jesus' graveyard I swear 60 years ago they woulda been shushed for such unbecoming behavior. That kinda thing was just unacceptable back in the day, and if I weren't already so darn old and smelly, I'd be marchin' out on the streets again with the NAACP demandin' a change in this country. We may have come far for this day and age, Miss Janice, but for all your twitters and tweeters out there, a pot callin' a kettle black would nevah have stood a chance when I was your age.

Ahh, but that's neither here nor there, and I'm afraid my mind's playin' tricks on me again. It's almost time for the day nurse to come check on my vitals again so I'd best stay focused before they come and try to wheel me away for some blasted 'group activity'—probably some silly Chinese dancing or a kindergarten meet 'n greet. Heck, if I were a little child still in diapers I would be plum-terrified to look some swollen old cow like me in the face too—and I don't blame 'em. Every time the perky young nurses change my diapers I feel like I'm bein' babysat by some toddler.

I bet you're halfway through that bottle by now and pettin' your cat too—better call or text message that young man of yours to come help you to bed by the time you get to the end of this tragic tale. That is, if I can finish writin' it all before I join Jake up in heaven.

Now where was I?

Ahh yes, Joshua Jones.

After that day at the fair, I could scarce keep my mind off him. It's like somethin' came over me, like I had become possessed with the spirit, as those Pentecostals would say at Sunday School, and I started to make up all kinds of excuses to go to town with the hopes I'd see a wink of that Joshua Jones.

"Momma, Sally-belle's needin' me to help her hem her pageant dress for the show comin' up. May I visit her in town today?" Sally was a "Townie", livin' in one of those fancy suburban town homes, while my parents insisted we keep on lookin' after my grandparent's old farmhouse a few minutes jaunt from the outskirts of town.

"Didn't you go a-helpin' her just 2 days past, young lady?" Momma'd say. "How come she's wantin' all your attention all of a sudden?"

"Why, with this pageant fast approachin', she just wants to make sure all her clothes fit," I'd say with my fingers crossed behind my back; Sally says that if I do that, then I'm not really lyin' so God couldn't punish me for committin' a sin.

"Hmph," and Momma would purse her lips while the steam of the iron billowed around her face as she pressed and starched my father's white office shirts in the living room.

"Well, that Sally-belle's getting an awfully big head on her shoulders if she expects you to come runnin' to her beck 'n call every time she's in a crisis bigger than the size of a pin-prick. Run along then, but you'd best be home by supper or your father will be wonderin' why you're out so late."

I'd always make sure to contain my grin until I was out of eyesight, and then I'd break into a little skip as fast as my bloomers would let me, singin' a tune as my arms beat like wings carryin' me off towards some unbeknownst fantasy.

"What's gotten into ya lately, Eliza?" Sally would complain. "You're just not yourself these days. It's like you're love-drunk or something."

I'd dare not tell her a peep about my crush; Sally couldn't keep a secret if the FBI paid her to, and I was smart enough to realize she wouldn't approve. Why, just the other day when we purchased our penny candy at Ray's, she leaned over my shoulder in line at the counter and whispered indiscreetly in reference to Joshua, "Every time I see this boy at the counter, I just want to wrinkle my nose. He sure does reek like roadkill, don't ya think?"

"Shh," I elbowed her gently in the ribs and shot her a look of annoyance. "Don't be crass, Sally," I muttered back.

"Well, it's true," she hissed in return.

"That doesn't mean you have to go broadcastin' it to the whole of Pittsboro like you're a news special on Television," I retorted and nudged us forward in line. Truthfully, however, I didn't want Joshua to overhear and find offense—and perhaps, I worried—refrain from showin' any more special interest in me.

Thankfully, as it was, she was so wrapped up with her debutante meetings and rendezvous with Billy that I scarcely needed to say a word.

"You seem quieter than usual, Liza,' she started remarkin' in those days after the fair when we'd be sprawled out on her ruffled, white duvet looking through Vogue magazines or when we'd sit in front of her large vanity pluckin' our eyebrows or tryin' out different shades of lipstick. I would never dare mention it, but there was a part of me that envied her beautiful dresses and her private bathroom. Her parents even hired some colored folk to maintain the home. Sometimes I only felt purty because Sally was my friend, although, since my 16th birthday, my bust had grown, my hips had widened, and my mother was finally lettin' me play with makeup, so now I was enjoyin' my newfound social status and the way men young and old were startin' to speak to me.

Have you ever been in love, Janice, that is, young-puppy love? That first rush of romance bloomin' on your face like a bleedin' rose? Don't you say no, honey-pie, because if I recall accurately in my old age, you had a crush on that cute classmate of yours who played Mercutio, what was his name again, Tom-something or other? Your father may or may not have told me about that time you stumbled back home past your curfew after the cast party during your senior year smellin' like Camels and Heineken... Oh yes indeed, Janny, your father told me all about the tricks you pulled during your senior year of high school. He was so frazzled tryin' to handle you as a single dad that he had to come see his Momma for "advice". I swear I watched his hair fall out in handfuls by the time you graduated! He was so relieved you actually wanted to go to vet school that he told me he personally funded your college road trip himself—I think he was just glad you wanted to leave Pittsboro and see the world for yourself instead of stay at home till a strapped-up cowboy with a 10-gallon hat from Farmersonly.com came a-callin'.

And now that you've had a bite of the Big City life in Charlotte you've decided to come back to yer roots—how about that, missy? Bet you didn't think you would. And now, post-school, have all your dreams come true? Are you happy doin' what you're doin'?

Cuz mark my words, Janny, if you ain't happy with yourself now, by the time you're called to meet with God, you're gunna look back and wish you'd lived a life that was solely for your well-bein' rather than lettin' anyone else live it for ya. I did that, sugar lumps, and not a day goes by when I don't regret some of my choices.

So whatever you do when I'm no longer around to make sure you stay outta trouble anymore, well, all I pray is that you at least do what makes you truly happy.

"...Do what makes you truly happy." Granny's voice echoes in my head. Gosh, I don't think I've thought about 'true' happiness in a long while: my days have just turned into one steady blur of work and Nick, Nick and work. I like my job at Valley Vet, where I work part time, but the hours are limited and the pay's not great. I can't stand my second job as a hostess at Lil Winnies Bar and Diner, but hey, I get better tips after a night of bartending that I get in a weekly paycheck from the vet clinic.

I suppose I'm happy. This is the first apartment I've rented on my own since graduating vet school last year, and Rascal makes for a great roommate. And Nick is a sweetie. He's been a huge support—we knew one another in high school, our lives took us down separate paths, and we reconnected 6 months ago when we discovered that we both had relocated back to Pittsboro. He was in the same grade as my older brother, so he's known my family for years and was a familiar face in our house even after my parent's split up.

But truly happy? Oh, Granny, why'd you have to go bringing up that question? This story is supposed to be about you!

Sighing, I scoot Rascal off my lap and set the blanket aside, hoisting myself off the couch. I swerve a tad unsteadily as I stand upright.

"Happy," I jeer as I walk towards the kitchen. The linoleum floor creaks under my padded feet and the fluorescent lights flicker overhead. This apartment may have the reminiscent appearance of the 70s, but at least it's *mine*.

"And that makes me happy," I declare, yanking open the sticky freezer door hard enough to rattle the contents inside. Where is that dairy-free Coconut Dream I've been storing in here for emergency purposes? Ahh, there is the marble fudge container glimmering out at me. I suppose I should have eaten dinner first, but I'm too far down the rabbit hole to turn back now.

Retrieving my contraband and weaving my way back to my perch on the couch, I tuck my legs under my knees and dig in. Rascal assumes his regal position with a sniff and it's like my entire identity is wrapped up inside a child's blanket, leashed to a threadbare couch, managed by an old, half-deaf cat, and dictated by dairy-free dessert and the tick of a clock in the background reminding me of just how loud the silence can be.

Bugger, this doesn't feel so happy after all. In fact, it feels pretty lonely; I think I've felt this way ever since my parents split up and suddenly I had no mother to help me pick out a dress for prom, take pictures of me during graduation, or to whom I could confide when I lost my virginity in the stale, dirty dorm room during a one-night tryst during a college frat party freshman year. No one to talk to about the stress of vet school classes or the creepy biology teacher who kept inviting me to his house after class so he could help me 'study'.

I labored so hard in vet school just to hear an "I'm proud of you, Janny," from my mom, just to feel her approval. I sent her invites to my graduation and my party—nothing. I sent her newspaper clippings featuring photos and an interview of the clinic here in Pittsboro—no acknowledgement. In light of what felt like rejection, I turned to my career to nurture that empty space inside of myself—but in return, I think all I've been doing is 'filling time' so that I can numb out the feelings of inadequacy by making a name for myself in the vet industry. It's been working for a while now, but with Granny gone and no one to keep me company save for Rascal and a bottle of Zin, can I really look at myself now and say this is what happiness feels like?

This Coconut Dream sure does taste good though. Maybe I'll have some more of that and see if I can bring myself to continue reading Granny's letter.

You better still have some wine left over, baby girl, cuz this next part's gunna get as turbulent as a barge hurtling through an Atlantic hurricane. Or maybe you'd better grab a bowl of that ridiculous non-dairy dessert you vegetarians call "ice cream." I refuse to eat ice-cream that doesn't come from a cow, and you can't milk a coconut, that's for sure! It just ain't natural. I mean, have you ever seen a coconut growin' in North Carolina? And yet we have cows growin' every 10 yards in the south. And I don't understand how all those vegetarians say they 'eat local' when one look at their freezers reveals...

Well, ahem, I'll keep my opinions to myself, Janny, but just know that you can't call yourself a proper 'southern' girl if you eat the same ingredients I give to my rabbits—that is, if I raised rabbits!

Anyways, if you care to know, the nurse says my vitals look great for someone who eats an animal every day, so I should have enough oil in this here ole engine to squeak out a few more miles of this story for ya.

Well Janice, you know by now that I'm hopelessly in love with a boy the color of trouble and that there's not no other slick-haired clean-shaven young man that can detract my attention. After a few run-ins on the streets of town and several glances through the store window as I waltzed by hopin' he'd notice me in my bright yellow dresses and sun hats, my lucky break finally arrived.

"Eliza, I need you to do me a big favor today," Momma announced one day late in July. The air was so thick with humidity you could practically take a shower in it, and the roll of thunder could be heard in the distant hills. I was lying all ornery-like on the couch with wet towels draped over my face and legs while mother was tryin' to nurse my colicky baby brother back to health. "I need ya to run down to Ray's and refill a prescription for your brother's tummy. I just can't fathom takin' him anywhere with the state he's in. I'll write it down for ya, sugah pie, and I'll even give ya some extra nickels to purchase one of those magazines you and Sally always fight over."

That shot me up to my feet faster than if I had been struck by lightning.

"I'll go right now," I announced, and mother gave me an odd glance.

"A moment ago, you moaned that you couldn't get up if the Titanic sank on you," she remarked, shakin' her head. "Young ladies these days...well, let me grab you some change and that doctor's note so you can best be on your way, then."

Five minutes later I was scurryin' like a pill-bug down the road to town, anxious and eager to see Joshua Jones.

My hopes were high, and I was not disappointed. When that little bell overhead jingled as I entered the pharmacy, Joshua immediately looked up from the paper he was readin', a look of delight on his face.

"Well if it isn't the lovely miss Liza come to grace my presence on this slow, muggy day!"

"Good afternoon, Mr. Jones, I'm here with a prescription to fill for my Momma." Usually I'd pause amongst the aisles to pick out my favorite candies or read the latest tabloids, but with no one else in the store, my feet couldn't help but walk me right on up to the counter, lean over boldly (of course, my heart was beatin' so fast I swear a race car driver coulda heard it over the sound of his engine), and plop the prescription right down in front of Joshua Jones.

"My mother would like this refilled at your earliest convenience, please," I announced.

"Well, miss," his eyes sparkled and I dare say he could hear the thumpin' in my chest. "Folks don't seem to wanna leave their homes in this here weather, so I've naught a duty in the way. I'll get a-goin' on this right now."

"Thank you, Mr Jones."

"Call me Joshua, please."

"Thank you, J-Joshua," I stuttered.

Once he'd disappeared into the back of the store, I made my way to the frozen food section to pick out a popsicle or ice cream. Momma had given me enough spare change for both a magazine and a cool treat, so my eyes greedily searched for an ice cream cake roll or Klondike bar and immediately grabbed the first thing I saw. Then I picked up a copy of the latest Vogue; Sally would go bonkers to find out I had gotten a copy before her *subscription* had even arrived in the post.

Joshua returned from the back room to help me complete my purchases.

"That'll be $3.92, miss Liza. Shall I bag this all up for you?"

"That would be mighty kind of you, I replied, handin' over the crisply folded green paper bills my Poppa had brought home from his paycheck the other day. Joshua disappeared once more to wrap up my purchases, and while he was gone, I wondered again briefly if Poppa would ever let me make my own money one day; every time I'd bring it up, he'd tell me I needn't worry my pretty little head over such things because that's what a husband's for. Now that I'd done graduated school and knew my letters and some arithmetic, he said there was nothing more I needed to learn other than how to make a man happy and raise a fine, strappin' family.

Oh, but if I coulda had gone, Janny, I'd have gone to school to be a nurse! All the girls I knew were settlin' in town or goin' off to the military newlywed and married off. Jus' a handful were goin' to school to be teachers or nurses, and how I wished I coulda joined them. I'd have given anything to get out of tiny little Pittsboro and make somethin' of my life.

That's why I'm so glad you left even though you coulda stayed, twinkle toes. You always have had stars in your eyes, ever since I held you in my agin' arms for the first time. You're gunna do something with your life, and I'm proud of you.

Well anyways, to make a long story short, Joshua did finally return with my purchases, and I left the store with a newfound pep in my stride.

"Make sure you eat that cake roll afore it melts on you," he reminded me on my way out, "and stay cool as a cucumber today, miss Liza."

So I found me a spot on the Whites Only bench on Main Street, next to a Whites Only bubbler, and dug into my brown bag of goodies. As my fingers rummaged around looking for my cake roll, they brushed against what felt like a small piece of paper. Lo and behold, I pulled out a blue-lined, yellow sheet of paper folded neatly in a little wedge.

My hands started to sweat and my thighs stuck together like magnets. My fingers shook as I carefully opened the note, makin' sure no one was watchin' – but the streets of Pittsboro were drugged sound asleep by the summer heat wave slidin' through the valley.

Smoothin' out the sheet of parchment on my lap, my gaze took in the neat, square letters leanin' up on one another like lovers holdin' hands:

"There's a birch tree in an overgrown grove behind Fitzer Park. I shall be lunching there tomorrow at precisely noon. If you'd care to join me, I'd be much obliged to await your arrival. Look for a piece of red string tied on a bush indicating the entrance path, and follow that inside."

I would read and re-read that letter that night, Janny, my fingers liftin' the paper to my nose to inhale his subtle scent. I knew those words were just for me. Oh how they sent a thrill shootin' up my spine! I was very quiet that night and went to bed early, claimin' a headache from the heat. But lyin' in bed, my mind raced and my body tingled.

In some way or another, I was goin' to see Joshua Jones tomorrow—alone.

I have one last glass of Zinfandel left, and the tub of ice cream leaves ringlets of perspiration on the plastic coffee table. Rascal has since wandered off; I hear him munching on the organic Purina Nick insisted I buy him ever since I adopted him from the shelter.

Memories of Granny stem all the way back to early childhood. At every major life event, I remember her being there for us. With each memory that arises, I allow myself to shed a tear or laugh at granny's antics, remembering the way she held our family together in those first few years after The Divorce.

I remember the time she held my hand as I got my first tattoo on my 18th birthday. She moaned louder than I did!

Or the time she stepped at the state fair to volunteer to be in the pie-tossing contest. No one wanted to throw a pie at a 70-year-old southern lady dressed in her best sparkly, fringed cowgirl outfit.

Or the time she caught her first fish on a family camping trip to the Blue Mountains of Virginia and was so surprised that she lost her footing and fell over the side of the wooden canoe. My younger brother captured it all on his Iphone.

With each memory surfacing and releasing, I feel a little more whole, as if those emotions were filling in the gaps inside of me and softening my edges. This time, when I lift my glass to my lips, I pause before sipping slowly, savoring the bite.

"Cheers, Granny."

And I keep reading.

There exists a birch tree, tucked away from sight, lost from the outside world in a grove that's been long forgotten, left behind by progress.

The peelin' black and white bark smells like a sweet cherry, and the aroma reminds me of the fizzy pop I like to drink after church sometimes.

Sunlight dapples through the leaves and I swear by the Bible that if I had x-ray vision, I'd be able to see little Cupid's angels peekin' their rosy little cheeks through the branches. The sounds of town fade away in this grove, as if time moves in another form altogether, as if this glade were an invisible reality existin' between two worlds.

It is here among the branches and thistles, the overgrown grass and the lingerin' aroma from the bark ignitin' a heady rush like I've just drunk a gallon of sweet-tea, that I find myself riskin' a tooth and a neck in order to pursue the pleasures of my young teenage heart.

I wish I could remember every word we shared from the start, Janny, and that I could recall each encounter we ever had. Alas, after near seven decades, you'll find that time rips holes in your mind and heart, and not even the fadin' memories can stitch your world back together.

Methinks death has this way of playin' with you, child of mine. The older I get, the younger I feel, till I can no longer tell my lefts from my rights and I care not if I've showered or brushed my hair for the day.

I'm feelin' tired this morning, Janny. I woke up sometime in the middle of the night feeling numb all over, and my vision was right blurry. I tried to call for the nurse, but my mouth wouldn't work—and for anyone who knows me, they know my mouth *never* stops moving—so I just told myself it was probably my dinner and I went back to sleep.

I feel better this morning, but I'm havin' trouble recallin' certain words and faces, and my body feels heavy. My time is comin', Janny, but I can't go yet until I get this all outta me.

I better speed it up, then.

Like I mentioned, I wish I could remember every encounter Joshua and I had in this here sacred grove, but my memory works in chunks these days. I'm sure our first encounter was one full of nerves: red cheeks, palpitations in the chest, a fear of being discovered...

Sittin' on Joshua's grey picnic blanket and pluckin' pieces of leaves off my bodice...

The awkward glances and goofy hellos as we sat there feelin' so much but not sure where to start.

But just as the caterpillar morphs into the butterfly, so did we, breakin' free of our cocoons and openin' our wings.

It started with takin' our shoes off and tossin' them into the grass. Joshua would bring me wildflowers he'd collected on his walk over. I'd buy some candy from Ray's and share it with him. We'd sit on his gray blanket under the birch tree while we'd suck on sours and share bits and pieces of our lives with one another.

He'd tell me about his family, how his parents encouraged him to learn as much as he could, because some day, they told him, he'd get to live in a world where that was possible, a world they would never get to experience.

I told him about my family, how my father worked as City Clerk and how he wanted me to settle down and marry a nice boy in town.

He told me about his younger brother's accident in the tobacco field, how he lost a foot when the chopper rolled over it, how his family struggled to pay off the doctor's bills on the "black side of town."

But mostly he told me about his dreams, about how he'd go to University to study law and history if the south were ever desegregated. He was furious about the treatment of blacks in

Pittsboro, even though he hid his feelings well behind a mask of polite "how do you dos".

We were always careful to cover our tracks. The birch tree grove was completely surrounded by brambles, but we'd take turns leavin' and arrivin', one of us waiting behind for the other to get a few minute's head start.

Joshua would sneak away on his lunch break, and I'd find excuses to sneak off to town—though I'd always be back before Momma ever got suspicious. Truth be told, she was grateful for the help. I was the eldest daughter, and my Momma had my 3 little brothers to care for over summer school break. So when I started offering to run her errands and pick up the groceries, she gratefully accepted the help.

"Liza-belle," she'd tell me, "I don't know what's going on inside yer purty head of curls, but yer turnin' into such a helpful young lady. Yer father sure will be proud, and I mighty appreciate the help." And she'd give me money for my candies or magazines, and I'd always make sure to do as she asked after seein' Joshua.

One day I snuck into the grove after deliverin' Poppa's parcels to the post and immediately noticed somethin' odd about Joshua. He was sittin' with his back against the birch tree, his straw hat pulled low over his clean-shaven head, black eyes stormy. His hands were clenched into fists that rested upon khaki-covered knees, and his lunch pail sat unopened. The air in the grove felt charged, and just as quickly as I had burst into the grove with a grin on my face, ready to share a new treat with him, my smile slipped off my cheeks and I slowed to a walk.

Joshua looked up as I timidly approached.

"Howdy-do, Miss Eliza," he patted a spot on the gray picnic blanket for me to sit. "I was just lost in thought again. This here noggin thinks too hard sometimes, I fear." The storm travellin' over his dark, molasses features began to lift as his eyes traveled over my face. I had taken some time today to curl my lashes and pleat my shoulder length brown hair, and I had even ironed my polka dot blue and white dress.

If Momma had started noticing the increased attention I was givin' to my looks, she wasn't mentionin' it yet, but I knew it would only be a matter a time before she'd start askin' on about some boy. So I was mighty careful.

"Why miss Liza, you look downright purty today," Joshua Jones mentioned, and I found myself blushin' yet again as he took in my appearance. "Is there any reason you're dressed to the nines today? If I'd had known we'd be having a party, I woulda brought my dancing shoes."

He laughed, white teeth gleaming like the moon in a face as dark as midnight. I was outright findin' it hard to breathe sittin' so close to him on the blanket our bodies could almost touch. I took in his long eyelashes, his eyes so dark I could scarce locate his pupils. The scent of tobacco clouded my thinking, and I found myself leanin' in closer in a haze of curiosity mixed with innocence.

"Miss Eliza, I..." Joshua's eyes widened as he read my body language. "Well, it's just that you're a respectable lady and I don't want to go stirring up any more trouble than this town's already got by kissing you, even if I sure as heck do want to.. I just..."

Mark my words, Janny, I don't know what came over me on that lazy summer afternoon, but it must have been the sweet birch bark aroma swirlin' through the air or how I felt so grownup in my outfit that I .. well...

"Shhhh," I placed a finger over his lips, smiled, leaned forward, and planted a wet whopper right atop his mouth!

I pulled away as startled as a goose in huntin' season, plum mortified by my dreadfully unladylike behavior. If Momma had seen me, she'd a-taken a switch to my hide and taken away my candy money for a month at least!

"Joshua," I mumbled, "I apologize, I don't know what came over me just now..." I pulled back and made to leave. "That will nigh happen again," I remarked, but just as I started to push myself out off the blanket, a cool brown hand wrapped around my forearm.

"Wait. Don't go. Stay, please."

Next thing I know, I'm turned around, forehead pressed against Joshua's, and we're sittin' with our hands interlaced as simply as if this kinda thing was as natural as the Sabbath.

"Eliza, I..." Joshua's voice cracked. "<u>If</u> anything were to happen to you if I kiss you, I don't know what I'd do...I'd probably just disappear." My eyes had closed and I felt myself meltin' into his gravity.

"Joshua," I whispered, "I know the risks we're takin', and I promise on Jesus' birthright that I'll breathe narry a word of this place to any soul."

"You promise?"

"Till the crows fly backwards, I promise."

And then we're kissin', Janny, my very first kiss, and oh how we're kissin', like the world's stopped turnin' and the only thing that exists is the sound of the bees buzzin' in the birch branches overhead and the way our lips fumble at first, but then steady, deepen, release, and dive in again and again...

The sky opens from above and the sun shines its light on the holy and the sinners, the white folk and the negroes until there's no distinction between the two. I lost myself that day, Sweat Bean, under the shade of the birch tree, held in the arms of a boy the shade of sin and the touch of death... I lost myself, only to discover a whole world of wonder and magic in the touch of a hand on my check and the taste of longin' in my belly.

I might not remember all the details of my time with Joshua in those sweet short weeks of summer, child, but I assure you, even when you find yourself wearing Depends and getting wheel-chaired around like a baby on steroids, why, the only things worth rememberin' then will be those times you tasted freedom or felt God's angels rainin' their praises down upon ya through the touch of a new romance.

Hang on to those memories, Patty Cake, and you won't feel so alone when you're lyin' on your deathbed waiting to book the next available appointment with God.

Now I'm getting mighty tired, short cake. I'm a sit me down for a hearty snooze before the doc takes a gander at me. I told the grumpy ole nurse who waddles around like an ornery goose about last night, and she bout choked on her artichoke over lunch—muttered somethin' under her breath that sounded like "stroke", and said she'd call a doctor in right away.

I'm sure it's nothing to bother your britches about, just a little looksie over, but I s'pose the doctor knows best. Lord almighty, I just hope He knows when it's my time to go, I'd like it to be with as little fanfare as possible.

The day before Granny passed, the doctor called my father to tell him the news. She had been transferred from the group home in Pittsboro to Duke's hospital in Raleigh, after suffering a stroke. I had been working at the veterinary clinic when I received the call.

"Janny, it's your Granny. She's not in good shape," My dad's voice sounded shaky over the voicemail. I still regret never heading out of town to say goodbye to her. I had told myself she'd be fine, and that I'd make a point to go out over the weekend when I wasn't so busy with work.

And then, when I left work later the next day and saw several missed calls on my phone's screen as I left, I just *knew* that Granny was no longer with us. Something inside of my heart twinged when I heard his voice over the phone, "Janice, you're granny.. she's.. well.. call me back as soon as you can."

I remember stumbling through my apartment doorway in shock, tears blurring my vision. Remember crumpling to my knees in the center of my living room, my chest feeling like it was ripping in two. Remember crying out, "Why, Janny, why couldn't you just have walked out of work to spend Granny's last few moments on earth with her?"

The days following her death felt like a blur: helping my dad sift through boxes of Granny's old clothes, donating them to Goodwill or giving them away to friends. Staring at photos of our childhood as we created a photo collage for Granny's memorial. Sitting in the front row between my brothers and my father at her funeral held in the Pentecostal church she attended for over 50 years in Pittsboro, squeezing my father's hand as the minister reads Granny's last rites. Throwing flowers into Granny's grave before the gravediggers cover her casket with dirt.

A shooting stab pierces my heart, and for a moment, I clutch my blanket, squeeze my eyes together, and feel my head spin.

If only... if only...

If only I had said goodbye when I still had the time...

If only Granny had been able to share this story with me when she had still been alive...

If only I didn't take life so seriously all the time...

If only I didn't feel so bitter and lonely...

If only my mom hadn't left...

If only my parents had stayed together...

If only life played out just how we fantasized sometimes...

Would we be any better off?

I'm so close to the end of the story...I'm hoping I can hang in there without drifting off to sleep, and finish reading my grandmother's letter while there's still the living daylights in me.

Well Janny-loo, after I had experienced my Very First Kiss, the summer just started to fly on by. By early September, the heat had started to break, and cool gusts of air breezed through Pittsboro like a baby awoken from its slumber. If I could describe what that time was like, well, I'd say it was like a Rite of Passage, that last bittersweet summer of still tryin' to hang onto the whims of girlhood.

But those innocent, simple times would not last for much longer.

Sally never did win the summer beauty pageant in Raleigh, honey, but my did she give it her best shot in the face of some heavy competition from those fancy, upscale city girls. For all her flouncin', preenin', and prissin' around, her sweet Southern town looks paled in comparison to those haughty looks the girls from Raleigh Preparatory Academy gave her—like they'd just swallowed a vat of battery acid.

After that August affair, Sally gave up her beauty queen dreams and took to chasin' after Billy. And when he finally proposed to her, their courtship was serious, plain, and to the point.

They married in the basement of Pittsboro's antiquated Lutheran church with the hush-hush of a business deal three weeks later. Billy was set to ship off to Georgia at the end of September, and if Sally were to accompany him, they had to seal the deal promptly.

Dashed were Sally's childhood dreams of a luxurious summer wedding in a fancy garden, ridin' up to the pulpit on a beautiful white stallion while the eyes of hundreds of onlookers watched her father help her dismount and then lead her up red-carpeted stairs covered in white rose petals to where the handsome figure of her true love awaited her arrival...

Rather, as she tearfully accounted to me the day before her departure, "it was awful, Eliza, an absolute eye-sore," she sobbed in my arms. We sat on her bed surrounded by boxes and clothes strewn all across her room. I was tryin' to help her pack a little brown suitcase with just her essentials (almost an impossible endeavor given the size of Sally's walk-in closet, her shelves of shoes, and her drawers of make-up).

"There, there," I squeezed her tightly, "I'm sure it wasn't that bad."

"Oh Sally," she pulled away, wipin' her eyes on the back of her hand, mascara smearing across her cheeks, "you have no idea how drab it was," she sniffed. "It was stuffy and dark, the minister's voice about put me in a coma, and I could scarce breathe in my grandmother's itchy, sweaty, stained wedding dress. And Billy didn't even give me a nice ring—just this borin' silver weddin' band. Oh, it was a complete disaster!"

Sally burst into tears once more, spewin' like a leaky bubbler, and threw herself dramatically against her duvet pillows.

"Oh Sally," my hand reached out to pat her shoulders, caressin' her fine cotton shift with my dirt-stained fingernails. "I'm sure he'll give you a much nicer ring once he's saved up enough money from being in the military awhile."

"But it's not the same!" Sally wailed into her pillow. "What if I go with him and it's just dreadful down at the military camp, Liza? I don't know how to be a proper wife—oh, what if he expects me to cook and clean for him and have dinner on the table by the time he gets home from work? I've never had to do that before! Oh and Eliza, I'm going to be terribly lonely without you there...oh, what am I going to do..?"

Her voice faded away, and she sobbed so hard her shoulders shook under my hand. I didn't know what to say to comfort her—what if she was right? But I kept rubbin' her back, her pale white frame tremblin' like a willow, and my thoughts drifted to Joshua and I.

And what would happen to Joshua and I? I was foolin' myself silly if I expected our illicit meetings to continue through the fall. Tensions were growin' in town as the North continued to play their hand at passin' new laws pressin' the South to make changes in their "whites only" policies. Rumors were spreadin' that a group of men—mostly young white men Billy's age, roughly 20 to 25 years ole —were fixin' to take matters into their own hands if the Gov'ner of North Carolina didn't defend their rights in a timely enough manner.

I knew that the more I became involved with Joshua, the more dangerous it would become for him. Why, even the previous night, I had heard Poppa talkin' to Momma in the kitchen when they thought all us children had gone to bed. I was on my way back from the bathroom when I heard them say my name, so I stopped, pressed my side against the wall between the hallway and the kitchen, and strained to catch wind of their conversation.

"It's just not safe for Eliza to wander about unaccompanied in town anymore, Marguerite," I heard Poppa mutter in a low tone. "Why, the other day, the Constable came by City Hall, and told us that this new group of rebels has been seen postin' up flyers on the telephone poles around town advertisin' their meetings—says he talked with one of them—the Davidson's boy, to be exact, says they call themselves the 'Populist Klan for the People', say they settin' about to defend democracy and the White Man's civil freedoms as originally documented before the Civil War. Says that even the other week, the Sheriff was called out to the County to answer a civilian call. Apparently, there was a vandalizin' on an old abandoned barn—some of them damn boys gone wrote, 'Reclaim the Confederate' and 'Bring back the KKK'. It's gettin' downright dangerous in these parts, Marguerite, and I have the feelin' we ain't seen the worst of it yet."

"What do you propose, Jacob?" My mother whispered.

"I think we'd be best to send Eliza north to stay with my brother in Philadelphia come fall."

My mother gasped. I drew in a deep inhale and my eyes widened: *Joshua*, I immediately thought. *I can't leave him!*

"Are you sure, Jacob?" Mother asked under her breath.

"It's the only choice we have, Marguerite," Poppa responded. "I already spoke with Job, and he and Matilda have a room ready when we give the word. With their little ones, I'm sure they'll need the help. Besides, it's just until the immediate danger passes. If civil unrest breaks out, I don't want her gettin' exposed to it."

"I suppose you're right, Jacob," my mother concluded with a sigh. I felt my heart drop into my belly and my eyes well with unshed tears.

"We'll tell her tomorrow," was the last thing I heard Poppa say before I blindly trudged back to bed, my heart breakin', my mouth silently mutterin' the words 'no, no, no' over and over again. My summer of love was coming to a close.

"**O**h, but you will write me, won't you Eliza?" Sally's voice snapped me from my reverie, and I came back to her room, forcin' myself to pay attention to her again. Above us, the clack of hammers sounded as some colored carpenters worked on re-shinglin' the roof. Their dull racket droned in my head and imitated the poundin' that was already formin' behind my temples.

"But of course, Sally," I promised, "every week."

Sally turned onto her side to look at me, watery blue eyes bloodshot with tears, her little turned-up button-nose swollen pink. Her blonde hair lay limp with sweat and dried tears against her down pillow.

"Oh good," she sniffled and smiled weakly, the corners of her mouth liftin' up into a trembling crescent moon, "because I'm going to need somebody to share the latest gossip with and keep me up to date on all the newest releases of Vogue."

I laughed and grabbed her hand, pulling her back up to a seat, "Mark my word, I will. Come now, we haven't all day, and *somehow* we have to stuff your whole life into two suitcases by supper time."

Once more, Sally threw her arms around my waist and gave me a tight squeeze. "Oh thank you, 'Liza, you're an angel. What would I do without you..."

"Don't start cryin' again, or I might start sobbin' too," I warned, but squeezed her tightly back. "Don't you worry, everything's gunna work out just fine—you'll see. It'll all be ok."

Oh Janny, this next part just breaks my heart to put into words. 'Bout gives me a heart attack—but I've been holdin' on to it for so long that I just have to release my sin before the Lord takes me. I just hope Jesus' looking from up above and knows I never meant any harm—no siree, I might have not known any better, but I declare on my 52-year marriage to Jake that I nevah could have seen what was comin' next even if I had been in cahoots with the devil.

Sally left the next day in a tearful fit. I bid her and Billy goodbye at the train station with her family as they took off for Georgia haulin' naught but their namesake behind them. Sally was dressed in a demure brown pencil skirt and overcoat, her blonde curls hidden under a brown hat. Billy stood ramrod straight by her side, givin' me nothing but a curt nod of his head as they boarded the train.

"Make sure you write," was the last thing she said before they departed.

Little did I know that I'd never see Sally-belle again. All the letters I wrote her were returned months later with a note from the postmaster readin': "Address not located." And once I had moved up north to Philadelphia, anything she had written to me wouldn't have been forwarded.

I know all you Millennials are so used to instant messaging and the ease of contactin' anyone, anytime, anywhere around the globe through just a little contraption in your pocket, but I still remember the days when a hand-written letter took two weeks to arrive.

I couldn't even graduate the 5th grade without knowin' my cursive, but nowadays, no one's writin' with a pen and pencil in school anymore!

Bah humbug, I'm turning into a crochety old badger, aren't I, Jenny? I better bite my tongue and rein in my thoughts before they race outta control. Golly, now I haveta recall the gist of what I was tellin' you before it floats away again.

Oh yes, now I remember.

My parents had just told me the same day that I'd be shipped off on a train headed to Washington, DC the first week of October, and I had to get the word out to Joshua.

But once they told me, it became nigh impossible to sneak out to the birch tree alone. The days were tickin' down to a close, and with naught but a week remainin', my childish heart was growin' mighty desperate. I had to see him somehow.

So one day while Poppa was still at work and Momma had taken the boys to an afternoon social at the elementary school house, I decided to sneak out, Janny.

I tore down the street at a quarter to noon on my blue handlebar bike, legs flyin' like my bloomers were on fire. I biked around town to avoid the school, turned on the boulevard headed to Fitzer park, zipped past the oak-lined entrance, along the sidewalk skirtin' the edge of the block, followed the dirt path when the walkway ended, and eventually flung the bike off under the brambles when the path became too narrow to ride on.

By now I could crawl on my belly with my eyes closed I knew the path so well, so I crashed through the bushes behind the park, burstin' out into the birch tree clearing out of breath and covered in bits of leaves and brambles. Joshua was eatin' his bologna sandwich on the gray picnic blanket; he looked up, startled, and then broke into a grin the size of Texas.

"Well if it isn't my favorite little lady! I thought I'd scared you away!"

"Oh Joshua, Joshua," I dashed to his side, eyes fillin' with tears. "I woulda come sooner but my parents are forbiddin' me leave home alone, what with all the ruckus in town...as it is, I snuck out and can only stay for a quick minute." I let myself melt into his embrace, felt his solid, strong arms engulf me in a mountain of tenderness.

"Shhhh shh Liza-belle," his voice crooned in my ear as he pulled my head towards his chest. "It's ok, it's ok."

"Oh Joshua," now it was my turn to sob just like how Sally had the days prior. "It's not ok," I moaned, "my parents are bent on sendin' me away in just a few days time, and I fear I'll never see you again!" I heard his sharp intake of air, a low whistle between his two front teeth. His grip tightened.

"Where are they taking you?"

"Up North, to Philadelphia," I cry, "to stay with my relatives until the commotion dies down around here." The grove was quiet save for the chirps of finches and the occasional sniffle of my running nose on Joshua's plaid shirt. Then I had an idea.

"Come with me, Joshua," I whispered. "Why don't you come with me? Why, if you moved up North you could go to school like you've always wanted to and we could have a chance..." I pulled away in excitement and looked into his brooding eyes with my bright, shiny ones, "a chance at actually being together."

"Oh Liza-loo," Joshua used his favorite nickname for me, brushed away my tears with his thumb grazin' my cheekbones, "I don't have any money to follow you up North right now, and I can't leave my family behind like that. And if I did, well, I doubt the devil hisself could convince your family to let you date a *negro*," he practically spat the last word. My heart sank to my feet again.

"But I don't' want to lose you," I beg, hands reachin' for his.

"Oh sugar pie, you ain't gunna. I'ma wait right here until you get back. You are coming back at some point, are ya not?" he asked.

I nodded.

"So I'll just save up some money, and when you're a bit older, well, maybe then we can return to the North together. Liza, I...I..." Joshua looked down and fiddled with a thread of the blanket with one hand. "Liza, I love you. And I'm not going anywhere till the devil takes me hisself."

When he told me he loved me, it was as if the clouds had lifted and all was right with the world. It was like I just *knew* everything would be ok, Janny, and that love would save us all. I might have made plenty 'o mistakes in this here lifetime, Janny, and you will too, I'm sure, but after 85 years breathin' and eatin' on this chunk of rock swirlin' through space like a spinnin' dreidel, the greatest lesson I've learned is that Love may come in all shapes and sizes, but it's Love that holds everything together.. even when it feels like everything is fallin' apart.

Love is love, child of mine, and I loved your grandpappy no less than I loved Joshua, and just as much as I love you. So when I said those same words back to Joshua on our last afternoon under the birch tree together, I just knew in my heart of hearts that we'd always be connected no matter what happened. And it was love that helped me let go.

But then ... Janny, oh, but right at that moment ... there was a rustle in the undergrowth and the breaking of twigs under the heavy sound of a booted-heel. Joshua reeled his face away from mine as quickly as if he'd been slapped. Twistin' to look over my shoulder, I caught a flash of bright red flannel disappear, movin' quickly out of sight without a care of being heard nor seen. I suppose, lookin' back at that ill-fated moment, one that will be crystalized in my mind forever despite Doc saying I got dementia, it doesn't matter if we saw them or not—what mattered was that whomever they were had all they evidence they needed for us to know we had been caught red-handed.

"You need to leave—now," Joshua ordered, pushin' me away in fright. The whites of his eyes were visible and I could taste the sharp, metallic tang of fear floodin' my mouth.

"But Joshua..." I pleaded.

"Go, Eliza, <u>now</u>." He started gatherin' up his lunch pail and blanket swiftly, hurriedly. "Whomever it was may not have been able to see your face, so hopefully they won't be able to identify you. For your own sake, you must leave, now!" I slowly backed towards to the path leadin' away from the birch tree, tears streamin' down my face, stumblin' over stones and tree roots.

"But Joshua, when can I see you again..." I whimpered.

"Just go, Liza," Joshua said sadly and determinedly.

He refused to look at me anymore, even as I moaned, "I'm so sorry Joshua. I promise I never told anyone, not one word. I'm so so sorry..." and I turned and stumbled away, feelin' Shame color my vision orange and Grief cover my heart in a dark cloud of mourning. I thrashed my way clumsily through the undergrowth, branches yankin' strands of mouse-brown hair from my scalp, my whole body shakin' with guilt and fear.

"You fool, Eliza, you're such a fool." I blamed myself for leavin' my bike so carelessly exposed. Relocatin' my bike from where it lay, forlorn and recklessly abandoned, I struggled to pull myself onto the cycle and pedaled away from the once bewitched, now cursed birch tree and the last image of my beloved Joshua standin' defeated and alone with the look of horror on his face, knowin' our worst nightmare had come true.

I biked away unsteadily, knowin' I would never be able to return, knowin' that things would never be the same again.

By the next morning, the news had circulated all over town, and the townsfolk were in a frenzy of fear, anger, horror, and panic. The rumors spread like wildfire, and the town was in such a state that the mayor called for an emergency town hall community meeting that night for any concerned persons –one meeting for the colored folk, one meeting for the white folk.

By mid-afternoon, a full-on riot was occurrin' in the streets of downtown. The negroes were walkin' out of their jobs, they were bein' confronted by the rebel gang, those damned so-called Populist boys—threats were tossed about like a lit match—and before you knew it, fists were flyin' and rocks breakin' the glass storefront windows.

The police were called in to step between the two factions of mainly young to middle aged white and black men, and a mandatory arrest was set in place for anyone caught so much as threatenin' a person of a different color.

The town was in complete mayhem, an absolute disarray.

Oh. My. God.
    I think I'm going to be sick.
I lurch off the couch, shoving Rascal off my lap to a series
of protests and meows, and drunkenly claw my way to the

bathroom as quickly as I can, retching the contents of the last few hours into the toilet while I hold on for dear life.

My head spins and my stomach heaves violently again and again. But I can't stop; my stomach is so full of horror, revulsion, and rage that not even my own projectile will dispel this sense of overwhelming disbelief.

I cry in agony for the lost life of a young boy I never knew.

I cry for the heartbreak my Granny must have weathered for 70 years.

I grieve for all the other men and women who must have experienced this, this absolute man-slaughter of another human's life solely on the basis of skin color.

I cry until there's nothing left to give anymore.

And then I somehow pull myself up again, wash my hands, take off my soiled, alcohol-smelling, tear-stained Care Bare PJ shift. Tossing it in my hamper, I stumble shirtless back to the couch; Granny's letter has been tossed aside, papers flying everywhere. I leave them be and curl into a ball on the couch.

Reach for the phone.

Call Nick.

"Baby," I sniffle, "can you come over? I don't think I can finish Granny's letter alone."

And by the time he's arrived, I've redressed and cleaned up granny's letter, popped an Advil, am guzzling ice water, and have placed a cool washcloth over my forehead to help blunt the pain of my newly-born hangover.

And Nick—glorious Nick—takes one look at my disheveled figure, drops his backpack by the front door, kicks off his shoes, and envelops me in a big scrub-covered bear hug on the couch, where, safely wrapped within his burly, hairy arms, I feel sane enough to read the end of Granny's letter—and share the previous pages—with him.

Well, Janice, I never thought I'd be able to write this all down in one place, but there you have it. I did it. It's over and out, and I feel at peace in my heart havin' shared this with you. I'm sure this wasn't easy to read—if I were in your position, I'd probably be callin' a mental health hotline or passin' out drunk on a couch somewhere. And I wouldn't blame you one bit if you did.

All I ask of you now that you know such sensitive information, Janice, is to be shrewd when it comes to sharin' it with someone. I ain't even told your dad, your uncles, or any of your other relatives, but I trust the Lord that you'll share this with the right people when need be.

You always have been so smart and responsible, Janny, even when your Momma left—you handled that tough situation with so much maturity for such a young girl. You're wise beyond your years, sweetgums, but I just hope you remember to pause, breathe, and lighten up every once and a while.

Don't forget to enjoy your life while you can.

And for a long time, I couldn't.

For a long time after Joshua's death—no, murder—I walked around carryin' a mountain of guilt on my shoulders. I blamed myself for Joshua's death, and I couldn't move on until I finally learned to forgive myself—and even then, sometimes I have to remind myself that if Jesus can forgive me, then I must be good enough to forgive, too. So if ever you feel like you don't deserve all the good comin' your way girl, or if you're holdin' on to some deep layer of blame or guilt over something even like your parent's divorce—try on a little forgiveness and see how that'll change your appearance.

So you're probably wonderin': what happened next?

Well, the young men who came forward admittin' to their crimes claimed to be a part of the Populist Klan for the Peoples, and they swore they were only actin' on Klan's orders to follow up on reports they had received of accusations this young colored man had been forcin' himself on an innocent white victim.

At least, this was information Poppa relayed to me over the phone once I was up in Philly. After the discovery of Joshua's lynchin', my parents became so distraught that they sent me to my uncle's lickety split on the next train headed North. In the weeks that followed with trials underway that lasted through the fall, Poppa shared that insufficient evidence could be found to charge the men, as no young woman came forward presentin' information backin' their accusation, because that young woman—*me*—wasn't there.

And thankfully no one ever discovered it was me, includin' my parents.

So these young men were let off (most likely on account of some heavy financial bribin' from their families) without so much as a rap on the wrist and a court order to disband all membership meetings at once. The whole thing was bound up and buried under piles of records in the Pittsboro city hall in a matter of 3 months-time, and just like that, the town pushed the issue aside and attempted to move on as if nothing had ever transpired.

And I highly doubt you'd be able to find any proof of a case anywhere, honey, not unless you really dug deep into the records in person—and certainly nothing available on that big Google machine you young folk use in lieu of encyclopedias these days.

And the rest is history, my dear.

You know the rest of my tale – how I moved on, stayed in D.C.—oh, it hurt too much to even fathom returnin' to Pittsboro then—met Jake at an uncle's dinner party, and attempted to put the past behind me and move on with my life.

But oh Janice, even though I've made peace with God and Joshua in my soul, there are still times I recall those memories of a simpler time. Those long, lazy days under the birch tree explorin' what it was like to love and be loved by a boy for the first time, and I remember it as clearly as if it happened yesterday.

I have no regrets, Janice—at least, my only regret is not havin' shared this story with you sooner. But I have loved, child, my how I've loved, and I've been loved twofold in return—by Jake, by my children, and by my grandchildren.

Won't you come visit this weekend?

My energy is fadin' quickly, and I don't know how much longer I'll be able to stick around. These doctors keep checkin' in on me when I'm just tryin' to write you this letter or nap in front of the boob-tube, explainin' that they just have to prick my finger for a sample of blood or monitor my blood pressure yet again. I'm not gunna miss this stuffy old place, my dear, with Fred my bedridden roommate snorin' loudly during my mid-day soaps when I'm tryin' so hard to concentrate, or the way my dinner-mates chew so loudly with their mouths open that all their food falls back on their plates.

Nope, I'm ready to cheerfully wave this elder care home goodbye from the back of an ambulance when my time comes: I've about had it with all the nurses wanderin' about in their Donald Duck Scrubs and the smell of antiseptic maskin' the other resident's incontinent bladder leaks whenever they get excited and jump out of their chairs during chair yoga.

Besides, why should I go participate in something like chair yoga and even pretend to lift my arms over my head when I highly doubt I'm gunna need to use my arms to help me roll around in my grave once I'm six feet under?!

You're right, angel baby, I'm feelin' mighty cranky in my last few days left on this earth. I can feel my mind lettin' go of this place, feel the pace of this world start to leave me behind. I've said my goodbyes, signed my last legal documents, and sold my grandparent's farm after spendin' the last 50-odd years livin' there with Jake; now, the only thing left of my life is to wait for it to end.

That might sound cynical of me, darlin', but needn't you fear:

I am at peace now knowin' my truth has been revealed; I can die as cleanly as the slate I was born on whence I came into this world as a babe.

I'll be waitin', Janny, waitin' to be reunited with my beloved Joshua, my deceased Jake, and even, sugar plum, waitin' to welcome you home too.

All my love,

Forever your Granny,

Eliza Mabel Wilcock

May 13, 2012

The next morning, I awaken to the smell of bacon, eggs, toast, and dark-roast coffee Nick's cooking up. While I've slept in for the first time since graduating vet school, Nick's cooked me breakfast in bed.

"How ya feeling?" he asks over our morning Java. We're sitting on the veranda of my apartment patio, my slippered feet propped up on his lap, steam from my coffee mug wisping through my knotted hair. After finally getting to bed around midnight, I feel strangely calm—completely cleansed, almost as if I've been reborn, or as if something heavy and ominous has been dislodged from my very being.

"Like the wicked witch from the east in the Wizard of Oz right after the house fell on her and squashed her," I truthfully reply. Nick laughs, leans over and ruffles my mop of curls.

"Well, it can't be that bad if you're crackin' jokes," he remarks. After breakfast and a hot, scalding shower, I feel ready to face the world again...but there's something I must do first. Throwing on a pale-turquoise tank top and circling my still-damp hair into a bun on the top of my head, Nick and I hop into his car and head east.

Pittsboro may have radically grown since 1950, but the layout hasn't changed that much—and with the streets pretty well deserted on a Saturday morning, it doesn't take long to turn left on the boulevard leading to Fitzer Park.

While Nick stays in the car, I disembark and wander my way towards the back of the park. There's still a sign at the entrance reading, "Dedicated to the Municipal City of Pittsboro on this day, July 1st, 1950." Fitzer park hasn't changed one bit since.

At first I'm wondering if I'm just chasing after fool's gold. There's no way the path would still exist leading to that old grove—would it?? I poke around the backside of the park for a few minutes, following the sidewalk to the point where it drops off, imagining that I'm walking in Granny's shoes on my way to meet Joshua for lunch.

Just when I'm about to turn around and walk back towards the car the way I came, something stops me. Perhaps it's my intuition, or the hand of Grace, or the ghost of my grandmother guiding me, but I turn to my left and notice what appears to be an imprint in the overgrown bushes. *Could it be?*

My heart begins to race, palms become clammy. I push forward, brambles scratching at my forearms and reaching for my face. After a brief struggle, the bushes part ways, depositing me within a little grove that still looks and feels remotely like what Granny had experienced 70 years ago.

I've found the birch tree.

It's looking pretty healthy despite some wear and tear. Past visitors have covered the tree in graffiti and have carved their initial into the white flaky bark, and empty beer cans litter the grass around the base of the trunk. A huge limb has fallen off, from a storm most likely, leaving jagged edges that shriek like how Joshua must have sounded when he swung from that limb by just his broken neck.

The birch tree has withstood the test of time.

I approach the tree slowly, run my fingers over the prickly, peeling bark, imagine sitting across from a tall, lean, black boy on a gray picnic blanket, trading sours and stories.

I smile softly, tears welling up from a calm place within—one full of sadness and remorse—but also, acceptance and forgiveness.

"You've done good, Granny," And even though I'm not particularly religious, I whisper, "Rest in peace. Go with God, and may you find Joshua and all your loved ones there too."

A moment later, my phone rings.

Caller ID shows a picture of my dad.

I answer, knowing that if I don't, it will be impossible to reach him later since he never carries his phone on his person anyway. He's probably wanting to check in about dinner tonight—after all, tonight's the night he's going to introduce me to a woman he's been seeing for a little over a month now.

"Hey pop, what's up?" I answer, and we casually exchange pleasantries while I slide my back against the beautiful birch tree and sit cross-legged on the ground. "So, I only have a minute to chat—what are you calling about?" I ask when our conversation comes to a natural lull.

"Well Janny-loo, I've been meanin' to call you tonight but have just been procrastinatin'..." my dad falters, and I smile inwardly: 10 years since mom left and he's still embarrassed to talk about women with me. But this woman he's introducing me to tonight, Jennifer, sounds like a nice fit. I'm excited to meet her, and thrilled that my dad is moving on with his life—even with Granny's recent passing.

With a start, I realize that it's about time we all start moving forward—myself included.

"Sure dad, what's up?" I mindlessly pluck bits of leaves and dirt out of my hair and twirl long stalks of overgrown grass around my finger.

"Well, honey, I just wanted to give you a heads up about Jen so you wouldn't be so surprised when you and Nick meet her tonight." Never one to mince words, he blurts out, "Janny, the woman I'm seein' is African American."

And just like that, I start to laugh and cry as Love the aroma of Redemption releases her fragrance over my head, smelling like the sweet bark of a birch tree on a long, lazy summer afternoon.

Epilogue

"Nana, will you tell me a story?"

"Now sugah pie, I just read you a story!"

"One of your stories, Nana, please?"

"Sweet Jany, it's gettin' to be past your bedtime, and I don't want your father finding out I kept you up when he knows full well you have school come mornin'."

"But I want to stay up with you all night, nana!" Eight-year-old Janice snuggles deeper into her grandmother's embrace. Eliza pulls the covers a little tighter around them. Pauses for a moment. Sighs.

Says, "Tell ya what, Jany-loo. I'm gunna sing you a song I used to sing to your poppa back when he was just a lil boy."

"Oh nana, I promise I won't tell daddy a thing!" Janice's face is so earnest and open, light as the moon. Eliza laughs and kisses her forehead lightly.

"Don't you be minding that, young lady. Just so long as you promise me to do your best in school tomorrow," Eliza responds.

"Oh I will, Nana, I promise!"

"And practice your letterin' 'fore the Spelling Bee this Sunday at church."

"I promise, Nana, I promise I will!"

"Very well, now snuggle in and let me rock you to sleep, Janny dear." Janice lays her head on her grandmother's chest.

Closes her eyes. It's well past her bedtime and her eyes have been drooping ever since dinner. While Eliza begins to sing, voice the whisper of a luna moth's wings dancing under the full moon, her granddaughter's breath lengthens and deepens, deepens and lengthens.

And Eliza's voice floats and flits back through memories of a time long past.

"The ink is black, the page is white
Together we learn to read and write
A child is black, a child is white
The whole world looks upon the sight, a beautiful sight
And now a child can understand
That this is the law of all the land, all the land
The world is black, the world is white
It turns by day and then by night
A child is black, a child is white
Together they grow to see the light, to see the light
And now, at last, we plainly see
We'll have a dance of liberty, liberty
The world is black, the world is white
It turns by day and then by night
A child is black, a child is white
The whole world looks upon the sight, a beautiful sight"

Song credits: "Black and White" by Three Dog Night (1972)

Don't miss out!

Visit the website below and you can sign up to receive emails whenever Eve Elderwell publishes a new book. There's no charge and no obligation.

https://books2read.com/r/B-A-BQHZ-QOGLC

BOOKS 2 READ

Connecting independent readers to independent writers.

About the Author

Frequently found roaming the hills of the beautiful Columbia River Gorge where she calls home, Eve Elderwell is an aspiring author who loves trying her hand at penning novellas and short stories. When not remodeling her 1970s geodesic dome home or writing research reports for her day job, she's most often journaling, cooking, or thinking up another short story plot twist.

www.ingramcontent.com/pod-product-compliance
Lightning Source LLC
Chambersburg PA
CBHW061717130726

47996CB00006B/2356